To Pete, Mom, Dad, and Twink
—M.T.

To my daughter Nia "Super-Boo" Morrison
—F.M.

KEENA FORD, LAWMAKER

Tomorrow my class is going on the best field trip EVER. We are going to the United States Capitol! The United States Capitol is a big white building with a rounded then pointy top like a scoop of ice cream with a spoon sticking out of it. When we go to the United States Capitol we are going to meet a representative, which is even more important than a student council delegate. A representative is kind of like a president, except there are 435 representatives and only one president of the United States. And the president has to live in the White House, but representatives can live in whatever color house they want.

The representative we are meeting is named Representative Thomas. I am very excited to meet him because I have some ideas for new laws.

OTHER BOOKS YOU MAY ENJOY

Keena Ford

AND THE FIELD TRIP
MIX-UP

MELISSA THOMSON

pictures by
FRANK MORRISON

You won't be bored if you VOTE for Keena Ford

PUFFIN BOOKS
An Imprint of Penguin Group (USA) Inc.

PUFFIN BOOKS
Published by the Penguin Group
Penguin Young Readers Group, 345 Hudson Street, New York, New York 10014, U.S.A.
Penguin Group (Canada), 90 Eglinton Avenue East, Suite 700,
Toronto, Ontario, Canada M4P 2Y3 (a division of Pearson Penguin Canada Inc.)
Penguin Books Ltd, 80 Strand, London WC2R 0RL, England
Penguin Ireland, 25 St Stephen's Green, Dublin 2, Ireland (a division of Penguin Books Ltd)
Penguin Group (Australia), 250 Camberwell Road, Camberwell, Victoria 3124, Australia
(a division of Pearson Australia Group Pty Ltd)
Penguin Books India Pvt Ltd, 11 Community Centre,
Panchsheel Park, New Delhi - 110 017, India
Penguin Group (NZ), 67 Apollo Drive, Rosedale, North Shore 0632, New Zealand
(a division of Pearson New Zealand Ltd.)
Penguin Books (South Africa) (Pty) Ltd, 24 Sturdee Avenue,
Rosebank, Johannesburg 2196, South Africa

Registered Offices: Penguin Books Ltd, 80 Strand, London WC2R 0RL, England

First published in the United States of America by Dial Books for Young Readers,
a division of Penguin Young Readers Group, 2009
Published by Puffin Books, a division of Penguin Young Readers Group, 2010

29 30
CW
Text copyright © Melissa Thomson, 2009
Pictures copyright © Frank Morrison, 2009
All rights reserved

THE LIBRARY OF CONGRESS HAS CATALOGED THE DIAL EDITION AS FOLLOWS:
Thomson, Melissa, date.
Keena Ford and the field trip mix-up / by Melissa Thomson ;
pictures by Frank Morrison.
p. cm.
Summary: Keena and her second-grade class go on a field trip to the United States
Capitol where they meet a congressman and Keena makes a big impression,
which she documents in her new journal.
ISBN: 978-0-8037-3264-3 (hc)
[1. School field trips—Fiction. 2. United States Capitol (Washington, D.C.)—Fiction.
3. Schools—Fiction. 4. African Americans—Fiction. 5. Diaries—Fiction.]
I. Morrison, Frank, date. ill. II. Title.
PZ7.T37195Kd 2009
[Fic]—dc22 2008018438

Puffin Books ISBN 978-0-14-241572-6

Designed by Jasmin Rubero
Text set in Cochin

Printed in the United States of America

Keena ★ Ford

★ ★ ★ ★ ★ ★

AND THE FIELD TRIP
★ MIX-UP ★

WEDNESDAY, SEPTEMBER 29
10 A.M.

I'm Keena Ford, and I'm the most important person in this journal because it's MY journal. This is my second journal. I got a new journal because I wrote in the old one so much that I filled it right up.

I actually got my new journal a few

days before I finished my old one. I got it when we had to go to the bookstore so my brother, Brian, could get a thesaurus for middle school. I was very excited to go pick out Brian's thesaurus because I thought maybe it was a kind of dinosaur or a lizard, like a stegosaurus, which is the best kind of dinosaur. But it turns out a thesaurus is just a book of words that mean the same thing as other words. For example, some words that mean the same thing as "quiet" are "still," "restful," and "silent." I told these to Brian when I was reading out of his thesaurus in the bookstore and he told me in a very mean voice to be quiet.

I found out there is no other word for "thesaurus" in the thesaurus.

My new journal is so cool. It has a picture of clouds and rainbows and angels on the cover. Brian said, "There is no WAY I would ever write in a girly-looking journal like that." And I said, "Good, because it is not yours." I thought that was a pretty good one, but Brian just stuck his tongue out at me and then Dad said it was time to go. He drove us back to our apartment in Washington, DC, where we live with our mom during the week.

On the way to DC, we listened to the radio in Dad's car. We always listen to Dad's favorite radio station, which is

just talking and no music. I think it is about the news and how much traffic there is and stuff like that. Brian used to ask if we could listen to music, and Dad said that when Brian grows up and gets a job and buys his own car, he can listen to whatever radio station he wants. Brian calls Dad's radio station "I Know That's Radio," because when the radio people talk about the government or the news, Dad says, "I know that's right!" I Know That's Radio is really boring, but it is funny to hear Dad talk back to the radio people.

I am glad that I am starting my new journal today, because today is a VERY important day. It is the day of the class elections for student council! The kids on the student council are kind of like the bosses of school activities like the bake sale and Spaghetti Night. The kids on student council also get to go to meetings three times a year. And the meetings are RIGHT IN THE MIDDLE OF THE SCHOOL DAY. I know all about student council because this fifth grader named Lamont who walks me home was on student council last year.

Brian says that second graders are too little to be on student council, but what does he know? I think I will be a very good helper with the bake sale and

Spaghetti Night, and that is why I am running for student council. "Running" for student council doesn't mean you are really running on your two feet, it just means that you are trying out. There are three other people who are trying out, but only one of us gets to be on student council. The person who gets the most votes gets to be the delegate, and the person with the second-most votes gets to be the alternate, which means that they go to the meetings if the delegate gets the flu and has to stay home or is in time-out when it is time for the meeting. The other people who are running are Tiffany Harris, Shay Jackson, and Royann Jones.

Tiffany and Shay are best friends, and Royann is new this year.

If you want to be on student council, you have to make a poster saying why people should vote for you, and then you have to make a little speech about yourself. My best friend Eric came over last night to help me make my poster and write my speech. Eric lives in the apartment right above ours.

Eric is not in my class. He is in the second-grade class for boys. My class has all girls and no boys because our principal put boys and girls in different classrooms. Eric is not running for student council in his class, because his

friend Chad promised to give Eric two brownies on Friday if Eric wouldn't run against him.

My mom got a big piece of poster board for me. I put the poster board on the kitchen table, and I got my markers and crayons out of my art box. Eric and I stared at the poster board for a while. We were trying to think up what to write.

"Chad already brought his poster to my class," Eric said.

"What did it say?" I asked.

"It said, 'Vote for Chad and You will be Glad,'" Eric told me.

"Hmmm," I said. "We should think of

something that rhymes with Keena."

"Or Ford," Eric said. He got a piece of paper out of his backpack. "Let's make a list of ideas," he said. I started saying words that rhymed with my last name and Eric wrote them down. I said snored, sword, roared, scored, and ignored.

"Florida," Eric said.

"That doesn't really rhyme," I told him. We kept thinking.

"I've got it!" I said. "How about 'You won't be BORED if you vote for Keena FORD'?"

"I like it," Eric said.

We wrote the words carefully on the poster board. Then we drew a bunch of smiling kids. Eric drew one girl who was sleeping, then he crossed her out to show that people would NOT be bored if they voted for me. After drawing for almost one whole hour, Eric's dad called and said it was time for Eric to come home.

"Thank you for your help, Eric," I said.

"Your poster looks very good," he told me. "I think you will be the champion of the class election."

"Queen champion!" I said. "I hope so."

When it was time for bed I whispered my speech six times to myself. Then as I fell asleep I imagined what it would be like if I won. It would be so cool.

This morning I brought in my poster

and showed it to the class. I was the first person to give my speech. I was very nervous, and I couldn't really talk at first. "I . . . I . . ." I said. I looked out at my class and saw my friend Linny Berry. She gave me a thumbs-up, and I felt a little bit better. "I'm Keena Ford and I want to be YOUR student council person," I said. I pointed my finger when I said YOUR, which I had practiced. Then I talked about how I would be a good listener and try to stay out of time-out so that I could go to the student council meetings. I also talked about how I would be a good helper at Spaghetti Night.

Then Tiffany, Shay, and Royann

made their speeches. Tiffany said, "My name is Tiffany, with a <u>Y</u> at the end. <u>Y</u> should you vote for me? For one thing, I think we should have a tea party instead of a holiday festival."

Shay called out, "Hey! That's the stuff I was going to say!"

"Shhhh," Ms. Campbell said.

"But I read my speech to Tiffany on the phone and she just said all of my ideas," Shay said. Then she started to cry.

"Nuh-uh," Tiffany said. "I had already written my speech when I heard Shay's," she told Ms. Campbell.

Ms. Campbell told Shay that she was sure that Shay's speech was going to be very good, and that it was almost time for her to say it.

Tiffany said some more stuff, then Shay got up to give her speech. She had it written on little cards. She started with, "My name is Shay with a <u>Y</u> at the end. <u>Y</u> should you vote for me?" Then she started sniffing like she was going to cry. She sniffed through the whole rest of her speech.

I felt very sorry for Shay that Tiffany had copied her speech. But I still wanted to win the election.

Royann's speech was a lot like mine. She said she would listen to people's ideas because she wanted to make friends at her

new school. Her poster did not say anything that rhymed, but it looked very
neat. Royann is very good at drawing.

After Royann's speech, Ms. Campbell
gave each student a little piece of paper
called a ballot where we write down our
votes. I voted for myself, of course. Now
we are writing in our journals while Ms.
Campbell counts the votes. Every girl has a
journal, but mine is the only one with clouds
on it. And I am the only person who takes
my journal everywhere, like to music class
and to time-out class when I get in trouble.

Now Ms. Campbell is telling us to
close our journals. She smiled right at
me. I think I might be the champion!

4 P.M.

I am not the champion. Royann is the champion, and I am the runner-up. I was a little bit sad, but not too sad. I was happy for Royann. I want her to make new friends so she will like our school. And I am just glad that Tiffany did not win after she copied Shay's speech. Plus, I might get to help with the bake sale if Royann gets the flu.

When I got home after school, Mom told me she was very proud of me for being runner-up. And Brian gave me a high five!

8 P.M.

Tonight Mom, Brian, and I had Family Game Night. Usually when we have Family Game Night it's on Thursday, but Mom is not going to be here on Thursday night. She is going to North Carolina for three days because her friend Carolyn is getting married. My uncle Jay is staying with us tomorrow night, and on Friday after I go on a FIELD TRIP, I am going to Dad's for the weekend. And then after that it will just be my normal schedule, so I won't write it all out.

Brian and I have to take turns picking the game for Family Game Night. Tonight it was my turn to pick the game! We used to try to decide together, but sometimes we would end up arguing. That is because Brian always picks games that I will lose. He picks Jenga or Don't Break the Ice! and in those games if you drop the game parts or make them fall, you lose. There is not a winner, there is just a loser. And I am always the loser. So I do not like Brian's games.

The games I like are card games, like Old Maid or Go Fish. The only card game I don't like is 52-Card Pickup, which we played one time when Mom was out and Mrs. Carlito from next door was watching us. Brian came into my room and said, "Do you want to play 52-Card Pickup?" and I said, "Sure!" because like I said, I love card games. Then Brian took the cards out of the box and threw them in the air and they went EVERYWHERE in the room. And then Brian said, "Okay, now pick them up." And I was VERY mad, because that is not a game, it is a TRICK. And it's not nice to trick little kids. That's what I said to Mom when she came home and I told on Brian. And he got in a little bit of trouble for that one.

Anyway, tonight we did NOT play 52-Card Pickup, we played Uno. I picked

Uno because the rules are not that hard to follow, and you get to yell "UNO!!!" when you have only one card left. We played the game three times. Brian won one time and I won two times!! That meant I was the QUEEN CHAMPION of Family Game Night! I was very happy. After the game I went to my room and got a piece of paper out of my art box. I drew a picture of myself in a beautiful queen dress. At the top I wrote, "QUEEN CHAMPION KEENA," and I hung the picture on my bedroom door.

THURSDAY, SEPTEMBER 30
10 A.M.

Tomorrow my class is going on the best field trip EVER. We are going to the United States Capitol! The United States Capitol is a big white building with a rounded then pointy top like a scoop of ice cream with a spoon sticking out of it. When we go to the United States Capitol we are going

☆ ☆ 24 ☆ ☆

to meet a representative, which is even more important than a student council delegate. A representative is a lady or a man who makes rules for our whole country to follow. A representative is kind of like a president, except there are 435 representatives and only one president of the United States. And the president has to live in the White House, but representatives can live in whatever color house they want.

The representative we are meeting is named Representative Thomas. I am very excited to meet him because I have some ideas for new laws. One of my new laws would be that in schools all over the country, kids have to take turns being at the end of the line.

In first grade, everyone wanted to be the line leader. But in second grade it's MUCH cooler to be at the very end of the line. Ms. Campbell calls the person at the end of the line the "caboose," because that is the word for the last car on a train. It's more fun to be the caboose than to be some stupid car in the middle of the train that doesn't even have a good name.

I have been the caboose only one time. Tiffany Harris gets to be the caboose a LOT. That's because she moves slowly on purpose. When Ms. Campbell calls on

Tiffany to line up, she always waits until the last second to move. Then she can always find some reason why she isn't in line yet. So Ms. Campbell tells other people to hurry up and get in line, and then Tiffany gets to be the caboose.

It happened today when we were lining up for lunch. I was trying to put my reading book away very, very slowly so that Ms. Campbell wouldn't think I was ready and call me too early. Finally the only people left at the desks were my friend Linny Berry, Tiffany Harris, and me. Linny sat up with her hands folded, and Ms. Campbell called on her to line up. Linny doesn't care about being the caboose. But I DO. And Tiffany always ruins it for me.

After Linny got in line, Ms. Campbell called Tiffany to get in line. And I thought, Yes! I get to be the caboose. But Tiffany started walking really, really slowly, barely moving her feet with each step. Ms. Campbell called on me to line up. I started walking really, really slowly too. Tiffany and I were moving like two old turtles. Ms. Campbell just looked at us and said, "Let's GO, ladies." So we started to move a little bit faster. We were almost to the line, and I was still behind Tiffany. Then Tiffany said, "Oops! I forgot to get my apple out of my desk."

Ms. Campbell said, "Hurry up and get it, Tiffany. Keena, please get in line."

So I had to get in line while Tiffany got her apple. And that meant that Tiffany got to be the caboose LIKE ALWAYS.

And that's why we need a new law.

5 P.M.

Mom braided my hair for the big field trip tomorrow. She put ponytail holders in my hair on each side of my head. Then she made two thick braids. At the end of the braids she put rubber bands—then she put barrettes that say "I ♡ my teacher." I got in a little bit of trouble with my teacher a few weeks ago, so it doesn't hurt to try to make her happy. My hair looks so cute.

My mom left for North Carolina right after she finished my hair. She gave me a big hug and said she'd be back soon, but I still felt sad. So right after she left I called Eric. He said he'd come over so we could do our homework together. That should make me feel much better!

Eric's visit did NOT make me feel better.
In fact, it caused a big, big problem. But I
think I've solved the problem now.

When Eric came over we went out
on my apartment balcony to do our
homework in the Homework Hut. The
Homework Hut is an old refrigerator
box. The cool thing about the Homework Hut is that it has rules that are
different from the rules at school. At
school we have a rule that you CAN-
NOT chew gum in class. But you can
chew gum in the Homework Hut! Also

in school we are not allowed to write with a pen. But you know what? In the Homework Hut, you can write with a pen anytime you want.

So as we were starting our homework, Eric said, "I have a new rule for the Homework Hut."

"What is it?" I asked.

"You can snip in the air," he said.

I had no idea what he was talking about.

"I got in trouble with Ms. Hanson today," Eric explained. "With scissors. I snipped in the air. When we snip with scissors we are only allowed to snip paper. But I just started snipping for fun, so I got my name on the board."

"Well then," I said, "it is a new rule. In the Homework Hut, you can snip in the air!" I grabbed my scissors out of my backpack. I started snipping them. I got so excited that I crawled out of the Homework Hut and stood up on the balcony. I was snipping around in the air like crazy. "Snipping in the air is fun," I said to Eric. The scissors made a happy, scratchy metal sound.

Then the scissors made a "thwap!" sound. Like there was something between the blades of the scissors other than air. Then I heard a "thump" as something hit the railing of the balcony.

I looked at the railing. One of my beautiful, thick braids was bouncing over the edge. I reached for it, but I was not fast enough. I looked through the bars and watched my braid land on the roof of a green car that was parked in the alley.

I made an "aaaaaauuuurrrrr" sound. It was all I could say.

Eric poked his head out of the Homework Hut. "Uh-oh," he said. "You cut off your hair."

"Aaaauuuurrrrrrr," I said again. I reached up and touched the side of my head. The ponytail holder where my braid had started was still there, but right past

☆ ☆ 36 ☆ ☆

the ponytail holder was just a little stump of hair. Eric and I both stared down at my cut-off braid.

"Let's go get it," Eric said. I couldn't say anything. I was still in some kind of a shock. Then we heard a "vrrroooom" sound. The green car started to move. It turned a little bit to get around the car in front of it, then it just drove off with my braid still on the roof.

Eric and I stared at each other for a few minutes. I didn't even cry. My brain just felt frozen like a block of ice. Then my brain unfroze and I started to cry. Eric just patted me on the shoulder. "There, there," he said, like an old lady might say to a kid in a movie. I cried and cried and cried.

"What am I going to do now?" I said.

Eric looked very worried. Then all of a sudden he popped his eyes wide open. "Wait here. I'll be right back," he said. He stood up.

"Are you going to tell Uncle Jay?" I asked him.

"Nope," said Eric. "I think I have a plan." He left the Homework Hut.

I waited and waited for what felt like eleven hours. I just sat in the Homework Hut and stared at my scissors. Finally Eric came back. He was carrying a purse.

"I'm confused," I told him.

"This is Mrs. Carlito's purse," he explained. "I asked her if I could borrow a few things."

"I'm still confused," I said.

"Mrs. Carlito knits hats," Eric said.

"I know that," I told Eric. "But I can't wear a woolly hat on the field trip."

Then Eric pulled a big clump of black yarn out of the bag. "Ta-daaa!" he said. "You are not going to wear a hat. You are going to make a new braid. All we have to do is braid the yarn and then put the yarn braid under your ponytail holder. No one will ever know the difference. Do you know how to braid?"

"I think so," I said. I divided the yarn into three parts. I tried to make each part nice and thick. Eric fastened the three sections together with a rubber band. Then I wove the pieces together.

Eric stuck the end of the yarn braid under the ponytail holder so that the yarn braid covered up the stump of hair. Then he stepped back to look at it.

"It looks, um, nice," he said. "Well, I had better take this stuff back to Mrs. Carlito."

"What else was in the purse?" I asked him.

"Some glue, in case we needed it," Eric said. He grabbed his backpack too. "See you tomorrow, Keena."

I thanked Eric for helping me, and then I gathered up my stuff. I walked very, very quickly back to my room, and I looked in the mirror at my yarn braid. I got another "I ♡ my teacher" barrette out of the cabinet and attached it to the bottom of the yarn braid. I thought it looked pretty good, but I didn't know if I should show Uncle Jay, so I got ready for bed. I got in and out of the bathroom to brush my teeth without anyone seeing me, because I moved like a very fast invisible secret spy. Then I opened my bedroom door just a crack and hollered, "GOOD NIGHT, UNCLE JAY!!" before I got into bed and turned out the light.

FRIDAY, OCTOBER 1
9 A.M.

Something everyone should know about
yarn is that it looks different after you
sleep on it. When I woke up this morning
my yarn braid was kind of flat and
wrinkly. It didn't look like my real braid at
all, even after I tried to fix it. It looked
like the hair of this doll I saw in a movie

☆ ☆ 11 ☆ ☆

one time, when this girl was very, very poor, and she lived in an old barn. She had only this one very raggedy-looking doll that she loved more than anything in the world. The doll was made out of some string sewn onto a dried potato skin. Even if someone loved me more than anything in the world, I did not want to look like that old raggedy-looking potato doll. So I decided to cover my head. I went to Mom's room to look for a scarf. And guess what I found? I found a scarf that looked just like an American flag. I decided it would be perfect to wear to the United States Capitol. I tied the scarf around my head.

When I sat down for breakfast, Uncle Jay didn't say anything about my scarf. He just raised one eyebrow very high up on his forehead. "I'm going to the Capitol today," I told him. "And this scarf looks like the American flag." I watched Uncle Jay very carefully. He just raised his eyebrow again and went back to eating his cereal.

When I got to school, I told Ms. Campbell that my mom didn't get a chance to do my hair before she left and that I really, really wanted to wear my scarf to the Capitol. I think she felt sorry for me, so she said okay! Now all of the girls in my class are writing in journals while we are waiting for the bus to arrive.

I feel sort of bad that I said Mom didn't fix my hair, but at least I get to wear my scarf and everything is going to be fine. My friend Linny Berry said she thought my scarf looked really cool! This trip is still going to be the best ever.

4 P.M.

The field trip was NOT the best ever. It was the worst ever. I am never ever going back to the United States Capitol.

The trip started out okay. I liked the bus ride better than the last time I had been on the bus. The last time I rode the bus was on the first-grade trip to the pumpkin patch. I was the only person who did not get to pick a pumpkin to bring home on the bus because I had a little problem with a scarecrow. A scarecrow is like a giant fake man made of clothes stuffed with hay. A scarecrow is put on a stick. He is supposed to scare the birds away so they don't bother the pumpkins. In this movie called THE WIZARD OF OZ there is a scarecrow that is actually a REAL GUY, only he does not have a brain. So at the pumpkin patch I tugged on the scarecrow's sleeve to get his attention just in case he was real. Then all of a sudden there was HAY everywhere that had popped out of the scarecrow. The scarecrow was not real, and he was kind of ruined. So I did not get to pick a pumpkin and I was very sad on the bus ride home from that pumpkin patch.

Anyway, this bus ride was much better. I sat next to Linny Berry and we played tic-tac-toe. Mr. Lemon sat right behind us. Mr. Lemon is the time-out teacher and he came with us as a chaperon. A chaperon is a grown-up who watches you on a trip to make sure you don't get into trouble.

When we got to the Capitol, we had to get in a very straight and very quiet line. I was not the caboose, but Tiffany wasn't either. She was in line right in front of me.

We were supposed to be very, very silent as we walked into the building. Everyone was quiet except for this girl named Addy. She was wiggling and saying "U.S. Cap-i-tol, U.S. Cap-i-tol," over and over until Ms. Campbell gave her the scary eye and she got quiet, restful, and still like the rest of us.

We walked in the building and saw a long hallway with white walls and a very shiny floor. We went down the hall and went to the door to the representative's office. There was a big sign on the door that said REPRESENTATIVE PALMER THOMAS — MARYLAND. "Stand very quietly," Ms. Campbell told us for the 200th time. She peeked her head in the office and a lady came out.

"Hello, class," she said. "My name is Jean and I work for Congressman

☆ ☆ 52 ☆ ☆

Thomas. We are very excited that you have come to visit today."

I raised my hand.

"Yes, the young lady in the flag scarf," said Jean.

"Who is Congressman Thomas?" I asked. "I thought we were visiting Representative Thomas."

"A congressman is the same thing as a representative," Jean told me.

"Is it in the thesaurus?" I asked.

I heard a man laughing behind Jean. She looked over her shoulder. "And here he is!" she announced. She stepped to the side and a man walked into the hallway.

"Hello class," said Representative

Thomas. "Thank you for visiting today." He was wearing a suit and some black shoes that were very, very shiny. "Are you ready for your tour with Jean?" he asked. The other girls in my class started nodding their heads. I nodded my head very fast so he would know I was really excited. All that fast nodding made my scarf slip a little bit.

"Hey, what's that?" I heard Tiffany say beside me.

All of sudden she reached up and pulled my scarf!! It fell to the floor. I tried to reach up and cover my wrinkly yarn braid, but it was too late.

"What is that string for?" Tiffany said. It felt like everyone in that whole

hallway got very quiet and looked at me. "What happened to your hair?" she said even louder. Then she started to giggle.

I covered my eyes with my hands. That way I could not see everyone looking at me. There were tears all over my hands in about four seconds. I heard Ms. Campbell say, "Tiffany, that is enough" in a kind of voice that meant Tiffany better watch out. I didn't hear anyone else laughing. Then Jean started talking about the different office buildings and how the members of Congress go to the Capitol to vote on new laws.

I tried to listen, but I kept my hands over my face because the tears were still coming out. Then I felt someone touch me on the shoulder. I almost yelled, "Get offa me!" because I was so mad and sad, but I peeked through my fingers first to see who it was.

IT WAS REPRESENTATIVE THOMAS OF CONGRESS!

He said, "Ms. Campbell, may I please speak to this student in my office for a moment?"

I moved my hands from my eyes to see what Ms. Campbell would say. She nodded her head. So then I followed Representative Thomas into his office. And now I will just call him Rep Thomas because "Representative" takes a very long time to spell. Anyway, his office had a very big chair and lots of picture frames on the walls. Some of the frames had pictures of people shaking hands, and some of the frames just had pieces of paper with writing on them.

"What's your name?" is the first question that Rep Thomas asked me. "Um . . ." I said. I think I was kind of nervous, because I couldn't remember at first. "Um, Keena Ford," I finally said.

Then I started to get a tiny bit worried that maybe he was going to tell me that I could not go in the U.S. Capitol with only one real braid. "Keena," he said in a serious voice, "watch very carefully." I did not know what I was watching for, but I opened my eyes extra wide so he would know I was paying good attention. Then he reached up and touched his own hair. And he pulled on it right where his forehead ended and his hair started. AND IT LIFTED UP OFF HIS HEAD! One part of his hair just lifted straight up in one big clump. I was so confused. I think my mouth came open.

"This is not my real hair," explained Rep Thomas.

"That looked just like the way the corner of the carpet looks when I lift it up to hide candy wrappers under it," I said. Then I touched my yarn braid. "I cut off

my braid by accident," I said. "This is not my real hair either."

"I figured," said Rep Thomas. "I wanted to show you that not everyone's hair is perfect. I think you were very creative to make a new braid for yourself."

"Thank you very much," I said. Then I told him that my dad has a bald head and lives in Maryland, which is the state that elected Rep Thomas. And I told him about our elections for student council. "I wanted to be the delegate, but I did not win," I said. "I am just the runner-up."

"I did not win my first election," Rep Thomas told me. "You should try again next year."

"I will," I said. "I saved my poster."
Then I asked Rep Thomas if I could still
go on the tour.

"Of course!" Rep Thomas said. Then
do you know what he said? He said he
would go on the tour too! With his new
friend Keena Ford!

THAT IS ME. I was very excited that
Rep Thomas called me his friend.

When we came back into the hallway,
Jean was giving stickers to all the kids
so that people would know we were there
for a tour and not just sneaking around.
Jean looked surprised and a little worried when Rep Thomas said he was going
to go on the tour too. Since Rep Thomas

knows the most about Congress, I don't know why he didn't just say the stuff on the tour instead of Jean. Maybe he made her say the tour for her own good. That is the same reason why grown-ups always make kids do stuff that the grown-ups could do by themselves.

The first place we went was UNDER-GROUND. There is a hallway that goes from the reps' offices to the Capitol, but it wasn't shiny like the office hallway. It just had lots of pipes and other people with stickers. We stood in a line beside a big toy of the Capitol in a glass case. When you make a toy building that doesn't do anything and no one can touch, it is called a "model." I guess they had the model of the Capitol so that if you had to wait in line for a long time underground you wouldn't forget what it looks like on the outside.

While we were waiting in line, Jean started explaining some stuff to us about Congress. She said there are two kinds of people in Congress: senators and representatives. They have different meeting spots, and only the senators get their own desks. And the senators can scratch their names into their desks without even getting punished.

After we got our stickers checked, we walked down another very long hallway and up some stairs into the real Capitol. We saw a big staircase on one side and some HUGE metal doors against the wall on the other side. The metal doors had tiny people carved into them. Jean told us that the doors were made of bronze and that they used to be in the circle part of the Capitol but that they were too heavy for people to open. So now they are on the lower floor of the Capitol, and if you opened the bronze doors you would just walk into the wall.

We walked up another bunch of stairs into the circle part of the Capitol called the rotunda. The ceiling had a very beautiful painting on it. It had angels and clouds and rainbows, which are my favorite things to have in a picture because they are on the cover of my new journal. The painting also had George Washington, the first president of the United States. George Washington is not on the cover of my journal, but I think I am going to draw him on there. Jean said it took the artist eleven months to paint the painting on the ceiling!

We walked around and looked at a bunch of paintings and statues. Jean showed us a painting of when the Declaration of Independence was signed. The Declaration of Independence is a big

yellowy piece of paper that we sent to England to tell them we did not want them to be the boss of the United States anymore. This was a LONG, LONG time ago. In the picture there were a bunch of guys. Two of the guys are George Washington and John Adams. And in the picture George Washington is stepping on the foot of John Adams! On purpose! I looked around for Rep Thomas to ask him if George Washington got in big trouble for that one, but he was talking to Tiffany.

I did not like it that Tiffany was trying to be friends with my new friend Rep Thomas.

"Okay, girls," I heard Jean say. "It's time to move to the next room." We followed Jean into a place called the Statutory Hall. There are many statues in that room. My favorite statue is of the first king of Hawaii. The statue is very big, and the king is wrapped up in a kind of cape. And you know what? His cape is made of SOLID GOLD!! Jean said that the statue had to be in the corner of the room because it was so heavy, if they put it in the middle it would fall right through the floor.

I was going to ask Rep Thomas why they kept putting these heavy things in the Capitol that had to go against the wall, but this time he was talking to Addy and Royann.

Ms. Campbell said it was time to line up to go back downstairs so we could visit another part of the Capitol. Once again LIKE USUAL I was stuck in the middle of the line. We were lined up at the top of a staircase, in a narrow hallway between two columns. "Be VERY careful on this staircase," Ms. Campbell warned.

"Uh-oh," I heard Tiffany say behind me. "I need to tie my shoe."

"Well, step out of line and tie it," Ms. Campbell said to Tiffany. "Just don't fall behind."

Tiffany was going to be the caboose AGAIN! I just knew it!

We walked down about six more steps. I was trying to be very careful like Ms. Campbell said. Addy was in line right behind me. She said, "This is the best field trip ever! Representative Thomas said I was his new friend Addy Smith."

"And I'm his new friend <u>Delegate</u> Jones!" Royann said.

When Royann and Addy said those things, it made me feel a little bit jealous. I felt like I was not Rep Thomas's most special new friend. He probably did not even remember my name now that he had made so many other friends.

All of a sudden I really, really needed to be the caboose. I was so sick and tired of being in the stupid middle of the stupid line. I decided to move fast so Ms. Campbell wouldn't notice. When we were about six steps from the bottom, I let go of the handrail and turned around super fast to run up the stairs.

The only problem was I didn't know that someone seemed to be walking down the stairs right in the spot where I was trying to move. I stomped on a shiny shoe, just like George Washington. And I slammed into the person's leg because I was trying to move so fast. And that person started to wobble and wobble.

And that person was Rep Thomas.

Before I knew what was happening, Rep Thomas had fallen on his backside. And I had fallen over too. I heard Rep Thomas say, "Oof!" and I said, "Whoa!!" And then I could feel that I was sliding. I felt my backside go bump, bump, bump, bump, bump, bump down those six steps. Then BOOM. Rep Thomas and I landed in a kind of a pile at the bottom of the stairs, right in front of the heavy bronze doors.

I turned my head and looked up. Beside the staircase was a sculpture of the head of George Washington. I felt like he was staring right at me. I felt like

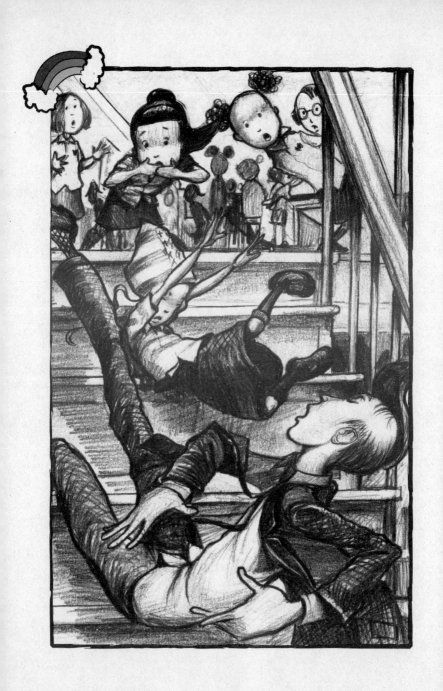

he was telling me that what I had done was way, way worse than stepping on someone's foot.

I looked back at the staircase. The whole rest of the line had stopped. I looked at Ms. Campbell. She looked pretty shocked. My next thought was that I had hurt Rep Thomas. I think my heart almost stopped beating. I looked at him to see if he was okay. He was kind of sitting up. "Oh my," he said.

All of a sudden I could see that some tall men in uniforms were standing around us. "Are you all right, sir?" they said to Rep Thomas.

"Oh, I'm just fine," said Rep Thomas.

"What about Keena Ford?" He and the tall men in uniforms were looking at me.

"I'm—I'm . . ." I started to say. Then I just started to cry again for a second time in one field trip. One of the tall men held out a hand to me. I just knew that he was going to take me right off to jail. I started crying harder.

"Don't be afraid," the uniform man said. "We just need to sit you down and make sure you are okay." Then I realized Mr. Lemon was beside me. "Are you hurt, Miss Ford?" he asked. I was crying so many tears that I started making a gulping sound, and I couldn't even answer, but I shook my head no. "Maybe we should sit down for a minute," he said. "I will go with you if you want." I nodded. Mr. Lemon told Ms. Campbell that we would meet them in the office building cafeteria later. She said okay. Mr. Lemon, the uniform men, Rep Thomas, and I walked away from the rest of the class.

Even though Mr. Lemon was with me, I felt very scared. And I felt very, very ashamed. I could not look at Rep Thomas. I could not believe that I had knocked over the representative. He probably thought I was the worst kid in the whole United States of America.

I followed the man in the uniform very quietly. He opened a door to a room with a long table and some chairs. Everyone sat down. The man in the uniform was talking to someone on a walkie-talkie. Then he pulled out a notepad and started writing some stuff with a pen.

My face was frowning in a very heavy way, like there was a weight pulling my bottom lip. I finally looked over at Rep Thomas. "I'm sorry," I said, and I started crying again. "I wanted to be the caboose," I said. "And I did not listen to Ms. Campbell. She said to be very careful, and I did not listen. And now I will have to go to jail," I said. There were lots of tears coming down my face, and I started gulping some more.

Rep Thomas looked surprised when I said that. "Keena, you do not have to go to jail," he said.

"I thought if you hurt a representative, then you had to go in front of a judge and he puts you in jail," I told him.

"But I'm not hurt," pointed out Rep Thomas. "And you didn't do it on purpose. But maybe you should just keep your place in line next time." Rep Thomas was smiling when he said that.

I looked at Mr. Lemon. He was NOT smiling. "Keena, why did you want to be the caboose so badly?" he asked.

I told him that the caboose was the best car on the train and that Tiffany always got to be the caboose. Then I said that I felt a little bit mad that everyone else got to be friends with Rep Thomas. And I told him that I had been afraid that he did not remember my name.

"Of course I remember your name, Keena Ford," said Rep Thomas. "And you can be sure that I will never, ever forget it. Did you know we had a president with the last name Ford?"

"A president of the United States?" I asked.

"Yes," said Rep Thomas.

"Oh. That is very interesting," I said. I tried to not sound disappointed. I wanted to be the very first President Ford.

"What is this room we are in?" I asked Rep Thomas. "Is this like time-out for kids who are bad on the tour?"

Rep Thomas laughed. "It's kind of like time-out," he said. "This is a room where the Speaker of the House tells the representatives to go when they are talking too much."

I looked at the man in the uniform. He had finished writing on his notepad and put it back in his pocket. "Well, sir, I have finished my report," he told Rep Thomas. "Would like for me to escort you to your office?"

"No, thank you. I will walk with Keena and Mr. Lemon."

We all stood up to leave the kind of time-out room. I was very careful to stay far away from Rep Thomas. We walked all the way back to the office building. I didn't look around at any of the stuff in the Capitol or underground. I just made sure that I did not bump into anyone.

By the time we got back to the office cafeteria, the class was already eating lunch. When they saw me, they all got very quiet except for Addy. Addy said, "I told you she did not go to jail!" and she was looking at Tiffany when she said it. Ms. Campbell handed my lunch tray to me and told me to take a seat. There was only one empty seat at the table. And guess where it was?

It was right next to TIFFANY HAR-RIS.

"I am not hungry," I said to Ms. Campbell.

Ms. Campbell looked at me. She looked at me like maybe she was a little bit tired. She also looked like she really, really wanted me to sit down. So I did.

Tiffany raised her hand.

"Yes, Tiffany?" Ms. Campbell said.

"May I please move?" she asked. "I am afraid Keena is going to push me out of my chair, since she knocked over Representative Thomas."

When Tiffany said that, I felt VERY mad. Tiffany knew that I did not mean to knock over Rep Thomas.

"Tiffany, don't be silly," said Ms. Campbell.

"Why are you being so mean to Keena?" said Linny. "She did not do anything to you."

"I'm not being mean," Tiffany said.

"Yes you are," Royann told her. "You laughed at Keena's hair, and that was not nice."

"Thank you, Delegate Jones," I said. I knew Royann would be a good delegate if she could stand up to a meanie like Tiffany.

"Her hair had string in it. It looked funny," Tiffany said.

Then Linny started to say that she thought Tiffany looked like something. I think she was going to say a bad name. But when she said, "I think YOU look like . . ." I said, "Shhh." I did not want Linny to get in trouble.

Just then Ms. Campbell said it was time to go. She started calling people to line up. When she called me, she said, "Keena, I would like for you to walk with me. Also, you will sit beside me on the bus."

When we got on the bus, I sat in the second seat beside Ms. Campbell. I knew I had to say sorry for three very bad things I had done. 1. I had lied to Ms. Campbell about why I had to wear my scarf. 2. I had not followed directions when she told the class to be careful. 3. I made Rep Thomas fall down. I did not know where to start, so I was quiet for a long time.

Ms. Campbell started talking first. She said, "Keena, I know that you did not mean to hurt Representative Thomas. But I told you to be very careful on the stairs, and you did not follow directions. I will have to talk to your parents and to the principal about what happened. And I think you will have

to write an apology to Representative Thomas, don't you?"

"Yes," I said. Then I told Ms. Campbell that I was sorry that I did not behave. And I stayed very, very quiet for the rest of the bus ride.

When we got back to school, it was time to go home. Dad was there to pick me up. Ms. Campbell had to talk to him about what happened at the Capitol. Dad did not look too happy. When we got in the car, I told him the same apology I told Ms. Campbell. Then I told him about the election and the yarn braid and the scarf.

We got to the middle school to pick up Brian.

Brian got in the car. Then he said, "What happened to you, Yarn Head?"

"Keena had a little scissors trouble," Dad told him.

"Wow," Brian said. Then he said, "How was your field trip?"

I looked at Dad. He was not making any kind of face at all. He was just looking ahead, and his mouth was in a straight line.

"It was okay," I said.

I asked Dad to turn on the radio before Brian could ask me any more questions. The guy on the radio was talking about Congress! I actually knew what they were talking about on I Know That's

Radio! I tried to pay attention. They were saying some stuff about taxes. I didn't know what they were talking about. I was just listening for the radio guy to say "Congress" again. Then I would say "I know that's right!"

Then I heard the radio guy say something else about Congress. He said, "Visitors to the Capitol got a bit of a scare today when a member of the House of Representatives toppled down a flight of stairs! It seems that Palmer Thomas of Maryland was tripped by an elementary school student on a tour. Luckily no one was hurt."

"Oh my gosh!" Brian said. "Keena, did you see that happen?"

I was very quiet. Brian was quiet too. Then he said, "Uh-oh."

"Yeah," I said.

"Nuh-uh," Brian said in almost a whisper.

"It was an accident," I said.

"What HAPPENED?" Brian kind of shouted a little bit. He was not whispering now.

"Welllllllll," I said. "Well, I got very mad because I wanted to be at the end of the line." And right when I heard myself say that to Brian, I knew it sounded really, really dumb.

"Are you kidding?" Brian said. "Was there a pot of gold at the end of the line?"

"No," I said.

"Wait till MOM hears about this," Brian said.

"I'm sure your mother will understand that Keena has learned from her mistake," Dad said. "What did you learn, Keena?"

"I learned to stay in line where I am supposed to," I said. "And I learned that Tiffany Harris and I will never, ever get along." I told Brian about how mean Tiffany had been to me.

"But Tiffany didn't MAKE you run up the stairs," Brian pointed out.

"I know," I said.

"Poor Tiffany," Dad said.

"HUH?!" I said. "What do you mean?"

"She must be a very unhappy person," Dad told me. "No one who is very happy would have to spend so much time making other people feel bad."

I thought about that for one minute.

"So am I supposed to let her be mean to me?" I asked Dad.

"No," he said. "But I'll bet she stops bothering you if you ignore her. Does she say mean things to Linny too?"

"No," I said. "Because Linny doesn't care what Tiffany says."

"See?" Dad said.

I thought about my list of rhyming words for Student Council. I decided that whenever Tiffany was mean to me, I would imagine that I had a poster that said, "You are being IGNORED by Keena FORD." I would have to tell Eric about that one.

8 P.M.

I am in my room at Dad's house. During dinner, I told Dad and Brian all of the cool things Jean had told us about on the tour. I told them about going underground and the statue room and the painting on the ceiling. I decided that maybe someday I could go back in the Capitol after all. I would just stay far away from that staircase.

After dinner I wrote my apology letter to Rep Thomas. I used Brian's thesaurus so I could make my letter sound very smart. I wrote:

Beloved Rep Thomas,

   I am very exceedingly remorse-
ful for colliding with you on the
stairs and hurling you to the earth.
I yearn for you to pardon me for
my blunder. I offer assurance that
I will demonstrate more prudence
in the subsequent era.

Adoringly,
Keena Ford

I read my letter to Dad and Brian. Brian said, "That sounds really weird, Keena." And Dad said, "The thesaurus is more of a tool to remind you of words you already know. So you should probably just use your own words." Then he said I had a good vocabulary and that Rep Thomas would appreciate whatever I had to say, even if it didn't sound fancy. So I rewrote my letter like this:

Dear Rep Thomas,
I am sorry that I knocked you down the stairs. I hope you can forgive me. I promise that I will never ever be unsafe again

for the rest of my entire life.
And I will never tell anyone that
you have fake hair like a tiny
carpet.
Love,
Keena Ford

I read my new letter to Dad. He made a little choking sound when I got to the part about the fake hair, but then he said that my new letter sounded much more natural.

Next I am going to write a letter to Ms. Campbell, but before I do that, I am going to add George Washington to the

cover of my journal with the clouds, rainbows, and angels. Maybe his picture will remind me of the sculpture of his head. And that will remind me of falling down the stairs in the Capitol. And maybe that will remind me to follow directions whenever I look at my journal.

I will probably have to look at my journal a lot.

DON'T MISS KEENA'S OTHER ADVENTURE!

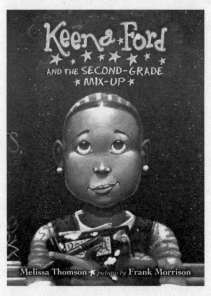